Man in the Mountain

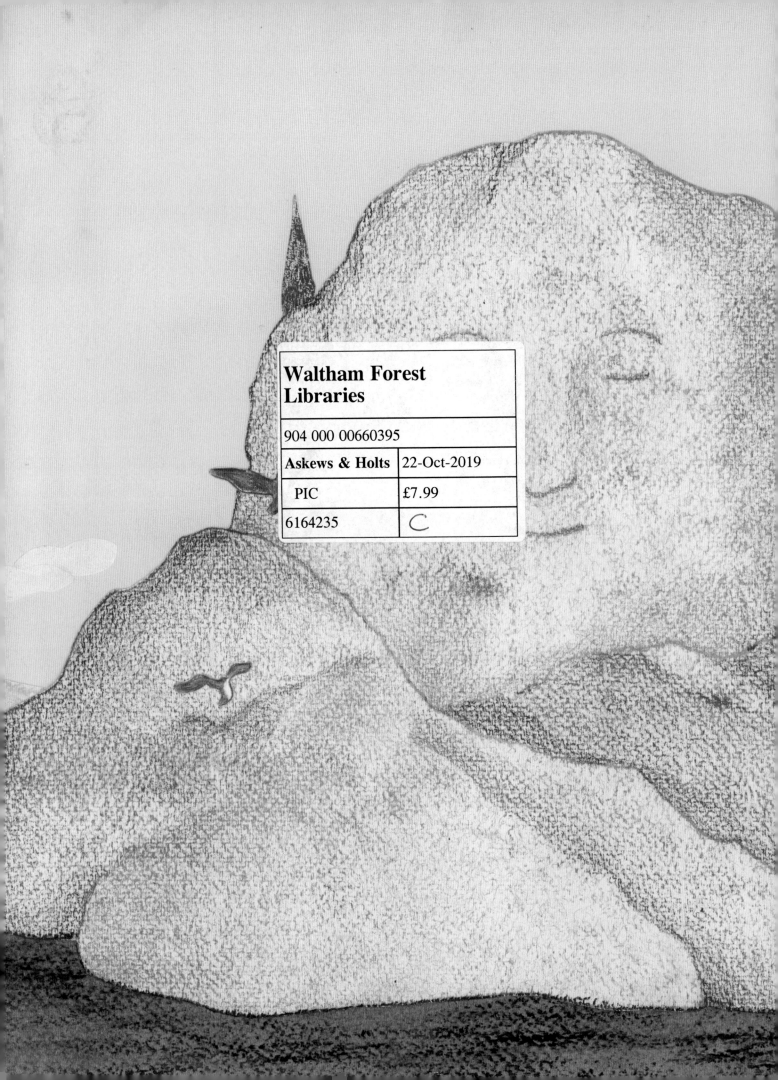

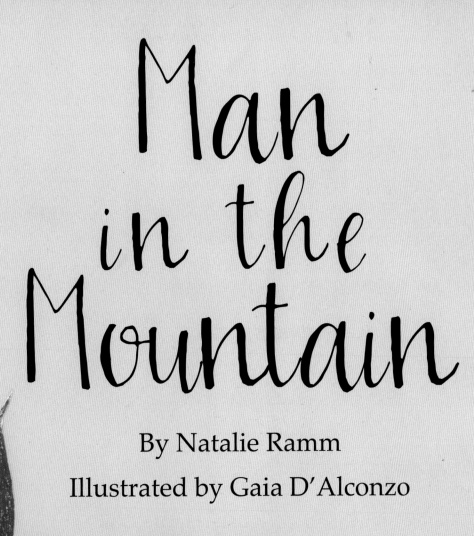

Man in the Mountain

By Natalie Ramm

Illustrated by Gaia D'Alconzo

Ragged Bears

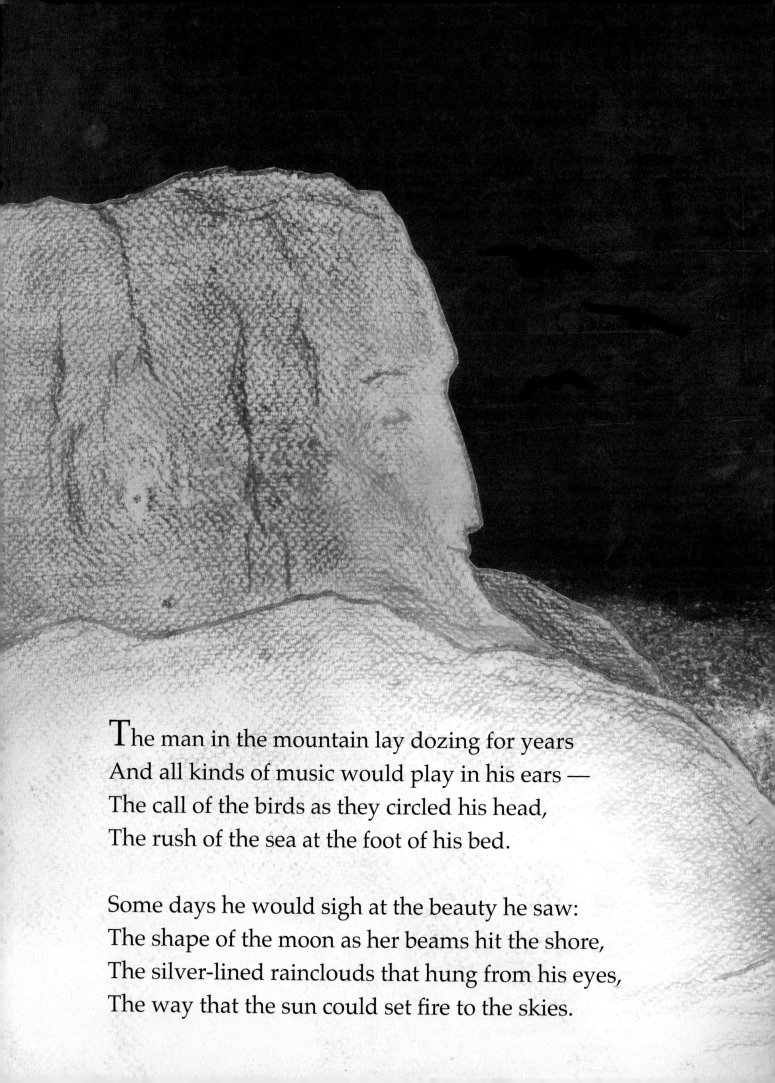

The man in the mountain lay dozing for years
And all kinds of music would play in his ears —
The call of the birds as they circled his head,
The rush of the sea at the foot of his bed.

Some days he would sigh at the beauty he saw:
The shape of the moon as her beams hit the shore,
The silver-lined rainclouds that hung from his eyes,
The way that the sun could set fire to the skies.

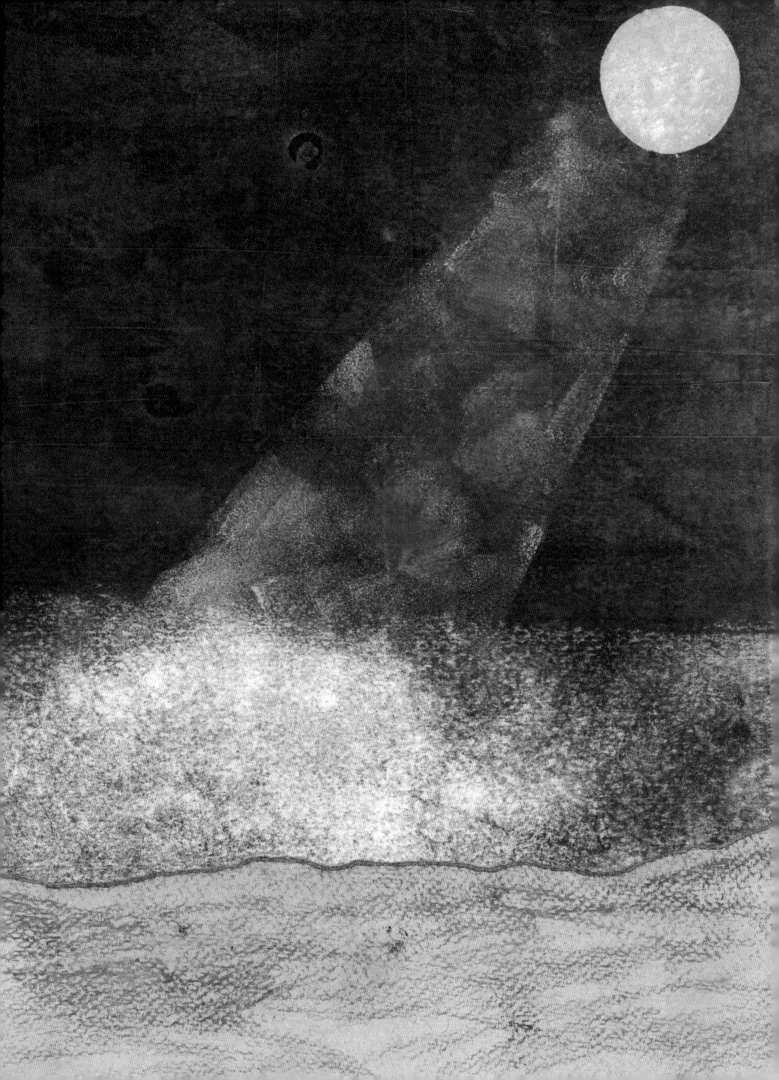

But he often felt sad, and started to cry,
And rivers of water would fall from his eyes.
They'd gush down the hillsides and stream through the trees,
And then the man's sadness would spread to the seas.

For the man in the mountain longed to see more
Than one single view, from one single shore.
But each time he started to lift up his head
The earth would start shaking, the sky would turn red…

The birds would cry out and the insects would freeze,
The sun would clutch fearfully onto the breeze,

The stars would go out and the clouds would all hide —
The man in the mountain felt so sad inside.

One day a small cuckoo called out from the plain:
"You're crying, dear mountain! I thought it was rain!"
So the mountain explained in his quietest voice,
"I don't want to be stuck here, yet I have no choice.

Oh cuckoo, the truth is I long to be free,
For the world is so wide, there's so much to see.
But whenever I move, I make the earth quake —
I feel so defeated I'm crying a lake!"

"My friend," said the bird, "I fly miles every day —
From Africa's plains I have flown all the way!
I'll perch on your shoulder and picture it all,
You'll see the whole world in the songs that I call."

So the mountain gave stage to the eloquent bird
Who sang of the wonders that she had observed:

Of bright Kenyan dawns where the lion cubs play,

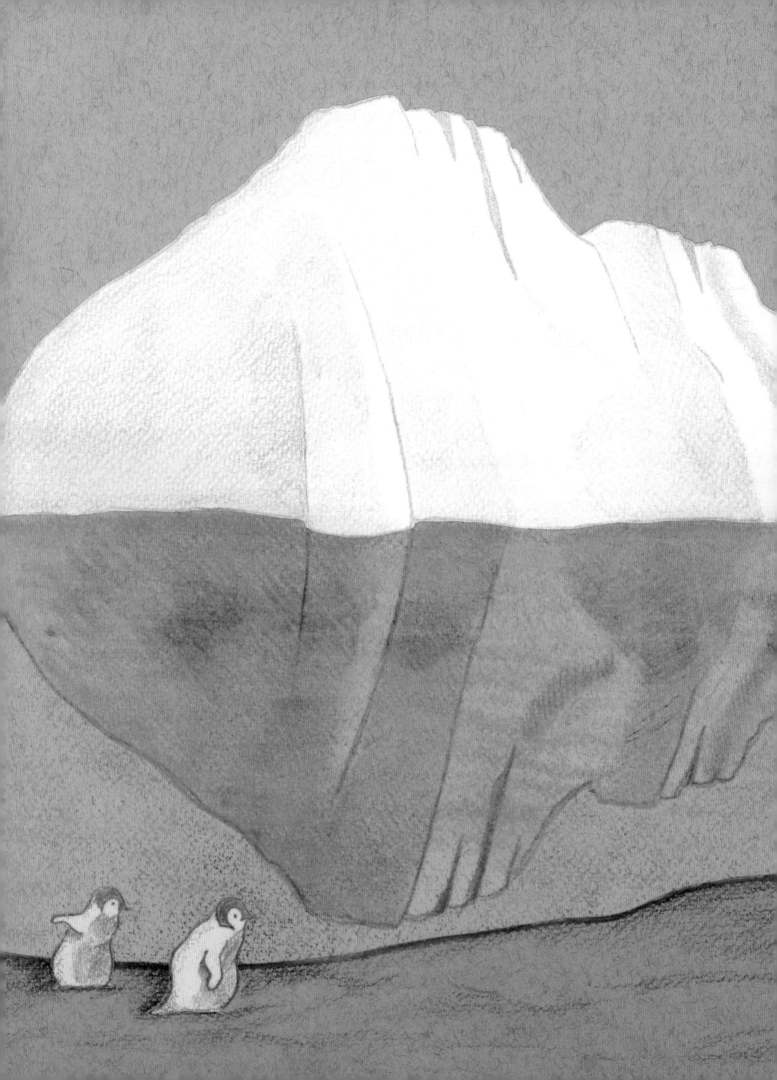

Of icebergs that drift in the warmth of the day,

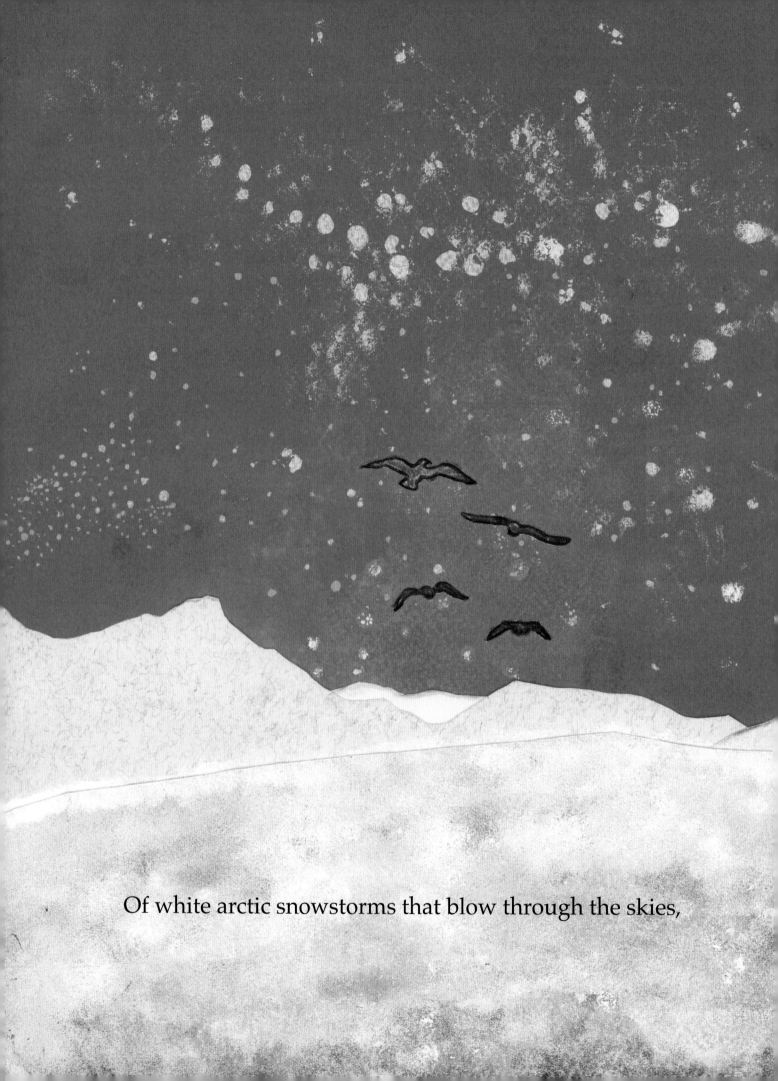

Of white arctic snowstorms that blow through the skies,

And Inuit children with dark shining eyes…

Of rainforest monkeys that swing through the trees
And bamboos that sway to the tune of the breeze,

Of Indian temples all carved out of stone,
Of Egypt's great pyramids…

…and statues in Rome.

As winter drew closer the bird would be gone,
Returning in spring with more tales in her song.

The man in the mountain now smiled ear to ear,
His world seemed so big when the cuckoo was near.
With eyes gently closed,
At last he could see —
The man in the mountain would always be free.

For my mum, dad and brother. And for Ben.
Natalie Ramm

This book is for my grandparents,
my parents & my brother.
Questo libro è per i miei nonni,
i miei genitori e mio fratello.
Gaia D'Alconzo

First published in 2019 by Ragged Bears Ltd., Sherborne, DT9 3PH
www.ragged-bears.co.uk

ISBN: 9781857144789

Text copyright © Natalie Ramm 2019
Illustrations © Gaia D'Alconzo 2019
Moral rights asserted

Printed in China on sustainably sourced paper

A CIP catalogue record for this book is available from the British Library